CHAIN OF SOULS

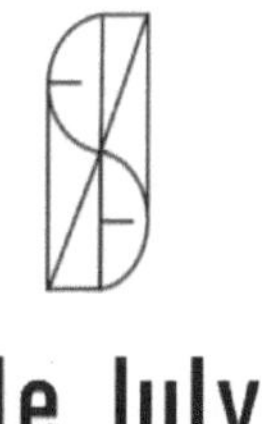

Edle Julve

CHAIN OF SOULS

ISBN: 978-3-4476-0132-0

Editing by Julio César Prado

Front cover image by Edle Julve

Contents

CHAIN OF SOULS

CHAIN OF SOULS

ONE

"Her last will has to mention a termination," replied the attorney, Mr. Chen. The man in front of him looked lost, with a gaze full of despair. The attorney found him attractive—not too tall, with a well-proportioned face, beautiful greenish eyes, curly light brown hair, and a funny mole on his right cheek.

"I'm aware of the law, but Elys didn't want a new host after her. She told me that so many times during our marriage," replicated George Martínez, annoyed by a legal technicality. He drank from the coffee that had been sitting for an hour. His lips tightened as he moved the mug to the side.

"I understand, Mr. Martínez." Mr. Chen crossed his fingers and lay over his comfortable chair. "However, I'm only allowed to open the will in the official reading. I'm not aware of its content. If your wife didn't express that decision in her will... You know the law," he sighed. "The host must leave a legal instrument, especially in this case, since she was one of the company's heirs. She had the right to petition and then undergo the mandatory process. If she chose a different path, I can't change that. I'm sorry."

George stood up and his face reflected on the coffee surface; his teeth clenched. Mr. Chen fixed his dark eyes on a screen with Ely's last will.

"After all, I suppose you are with them."

"I don't know what you mean, Mr. Martínez."

"I couldn't expect more. You follow their commands."

The man with whom he had a meeting glanced at him. Mr. Chen was the leading attorney of Exelis Labs. His slanted eyes seemed amused by George's outburst. During his career, he observed clients irritated by laws. He always spoke clearly and within the legal limits.

"I hope to see you tomorrow for the official reading of Mrs. Elys Sigman-Gold's will."

Without a word, George turned and exited the office. He was furious and took the elevator to leave the building. He hated everything about Exelis Labs. They disregarded Elys' last will, her actions and plans now she was gone.

They had a successful marriage, despite her meddling family. George and Elys lived far from them, and for seven years, both pretended she was not part of the Sigman-Gold family. They had two beautiful girls named Rita and Ellen, twins, who were now five years old. George was happy that they were too young to host, as Elys also did not want her children involved.

"George, promise me you'll keep our girls away from their madness. This must finish with me." Those words still echoed in George's mind. He left the elevator, opened the main doors, and started walking down the street.

After Ely's death, he moved to a small house in the city with his daughters. The old house they owned in the forest, near the town, conveyed sad memories—the chair where Elys fell asleep after a good glass of wine at night, the comfortable bed when they slept, cuddled, and made love. He even missed their minor disagreements, like his obsession with the kitchen towels and how Elys used them to dry her hands and the dishes, not respecting his categories.

The new house was small and cozy. It helped to avoid the constant memory of Elys in each corner, which made George vulnerable and unable to focus on his daughters. He understood there would be time to grieve her wife, but now he needed strength to fight for her last wish and defeat them.

"Mrs. Graciano, through her discovery, aimed to explore and understand what happens to the human conscience after death. Now, people have twisted that purpose into a commodity."

Joseph Maria Vera
The New Republic News
(2057)

TWO

George forgot his umbrella and got soaked by the heavy rain that caught him before reaching home. Elys was rich; he was not. George owned a small shoe workshop where he met her. She placed an order for a pair of sandals from his virtual store while she was on holiday. Elys belonged to the large northern country, while George belonged to the southern country, known for its abundant jungle and rain.as from the big northern country, and George belonged to the southern country, which was rich in jungle and rain. He used to make shoes as a hobby while Elys lived. The shoe business once again became their way of life and supporting the twins. George felt afraid that her family would take their children, his last bond with Elys, from him.

When he opened the door, he heard a familiar voice. After that, a laugh. The twins joined it. Then a clapping.

"Welcome home, master," greeted the synthetic in charge of his household. The ALO-3, a product of the International Robotic Industries (IRI), stood as a powerful creation. IRI discontinued the droid fifteen years ago. Ely's synthetic belonged to her during her teenage years, and she never parted with it, and since then, it has been serving them well.

"I order you to ban any stranger from accessing our house." George knew it was foolish to reprimand a synthetic, but he felt frustrated following Mr. Chen's meeting.

"Mr. Sigman-Gold is not unfamiliar. He's Mrs. Ely's brother," reasoned the android.

"Never mind..." groaned George and walked to the living room.

Hugo Sigman-Gold stood there, Ely's twin, dressed in an expensive suit, which provided a sharp contrast to George's modest clothes. Hugo represented the male version of Elys—tall, with dark ginger hair, fair skin sprinkled with freckles on his straight nose, and large brown eyes. However, the difference was in their smiles. Elys had a mischievous and beautiful smile, while Hugo had a wicked one, promising he had intentions of something awful every second. Hugo and George shared a mutual dislike from the beginning.

Hugo indulged in playing with his niece's toys, who inherited their mother's ginger hair but had greenish eyes, like their father. Rita and Ellen packed colorful blocks in a funny order, aiming to build a castle. The crooked construction fell off after Ellen put a heavy block on the top. The tiny demolition amused the sisters, and they clapped. Hugo joined them, celebrating the achievement with a wide smile.

"Hi, George," said Hugo, grinning, not with his eyes, and started putting the blocks in a big box.

"What are you doing here?"

"I wanted to visit my nieces, make sure they're doing ok."

"Are you implying I can't take care of them? Is that?" called out George.

The twin's laughter ceased, and their focus turned to their father. Rita started crying, and Ellen looked at her sister, amazed, but remained calm and focused on the remaining blocks. George took Rita in his arms and hugged her. "Sorry, darling..." he murmured in his daughter's ear.

"You're making them nervous with your evil intentions," added George, in desperation, kissing Rita on her cheek. "They don't need this, not after their mother... Please, don't bother us."

"They're my nieces, George... You can't stop me from visiting them." He reiterated as he stood up.

George knew he had no legal claim to keep them from him. He was their family, a powerful one.

"If you want to visit them, at least give me notice," said George, trying to calm himself.

"Perhaps Elys had distanced herself from me. She had reasons. But I've all the right to see my nieces. They're my family. Is that understood?"

"Give me notice... It's all I ask," George repeated, still hugging Rita, who ceased crying and started sobbing. Ellen made a new castle with cubes, ignoring everything around her and humming a song Elys used to sing for them before bed.

"I'll meet with you tomorrow, in Ely's will reading..."

With Rita's tiny arms around his neck, George closed his eyes until Hugo left the house. The song Ellen hummed echoed in the room, and George shed tears. The block castle fell off again.

"Creating a Symbiote is expensive and requires costly technology. It's estimated that there are around 1.500 symbiotes on Earth alone. About 300 in the outer colonies. The older ones are around 85 and may live over a thousand years."

Stephen Garnier
International Labs Statistics
(May 2069)

THREE

The reading was in one of the Exelis Labs' offices. Ely's parents were there, also Hugo, who was enjoying a glass of whiskey and looking through the wide window. Ely's mother, Estela, was a small plump woman with pale ginger gray hair, brown eyes, and fancy clothes. She stared at George with disdain when he entered the room. Ely's father, Raul, was tall with dark brown hair and cold gray eyes; he ignored George. The twins stayed home with the synthetic, as their presence wasn't necessarily because of their young age and the law did not require their presence. George preferred it that way because he knew Ely's family hostility towards him. The girls would cry, especially Rita, and he was not dealing with that after losing Elys.

"Good morning," greeted Mr. Chen. He came in and

gestured towards the elegant chairs by the desk. "Please, you may sit."

George chose a chair far from Ely's family. He could feel their loathing, like a dark energy coming from their gazes.

"As you know, Elys Sigman-Gold hosted the Exelis Labs symbiote, the fourth generation," stated Mr. Chen after sitting down. "As any host, under federal law, she had some privileges over the symbiote."

"Mr. Chen," retorted Estela, exasperated. "We know the law. We don't need a lecture on it... Please, read the will."

Mr. Chen grabbed a small seal on her finger that allowed him to open the will as the designated attorney.

"I, Elys Sigman-Gold, resident of Section 45, Street M5A2A2 East, being of sound mind, not acting under duress or undue influence, and understanding all my property and this disposition thereof, do at this moment make, publish, and declare this document to be my testament..." Mr. Chen read with a clear voice.

The testament was long. George received full custody of his daughters, the house in the forest, and money to support him for life. The twins inherited all of Ely's company shares, which was 53%, under the guardianship of her brother until they came of age. The rest was too technical, and Ely's family seemed pleased.

"Is there any mention of a termination?" urged George, anxious, when Mr. Chen finished the reading.

"How dare you?" blurted Raul, aghast.

"It was her last will. She told me many times..." George was furious.

"The biggest mistake my daughter made was marrying you," fulminated Estela. "You put those ridiculous 'ideas' in her mind..."

"She didn't want more hosts... Elys thought it was wrong, even evil," said George, as if he was immune to his mother-in-law's verbal attacks.

"Mr. Chen, is anything else in the will?" asked Hugo, in his usual practical tone.

"This is everything."

"We're done, then."

George tried to raise his voice while everybody was leaving. "The symbiote..."

"Consider yourself lucky, Martínez!" Interrupted Raul Sigman-Gold, looking at him. "My daughter was generous with you. She left you a fortune, my granddaughters' custody, and a beautiful house. What else do you want? Considering your situation, a shoemaker..."

"My girls have shoemaker blood too," countered George with a smile.

"They're Sigman-Gold just like her mother, and that is enough for us. Your contribution was... circumstantial," said Estela, too proud of her family lineage.

"What's going to happen with the symbiote?" asked George. Ely's parents ignored his question and walked out of the room. Hugo stayed and fixed his eyes on George's.

"I'm going to be the host," Hugo's lips curved behind the glass that was almost empty.

"The symbiote preserves the experiences and memories of the previous host, transferring them to the next body. A bridge for the soul to survive."

Dr. Susan Graciano
The Survival of Human Conscience
(2047)

FOUR

Hugo Sigman-Gold was now the heir of the symbiote. He was ecstatic. This was an event he coveted forever. Since the family designated all women as hosts from the beginning, her sister was the most likely member to carry the family inheritance. The first one was Silvia Gold, who created the symbiote, and only female relatives were suitable to carry it, a measure taken for the health of the symbiote. After Silvia arrived, Filippa, Amelia (one of his mother's sisters), and Elys; all mothers, daughters, or nieces joined. Among those women, they held the symbiote for almost one hundred years, bridging and keeping the company's knowledge and wealth through generations. Each new host used the experiences of the former ones, improving understanding of the company's business. Despite completing the required training a decade ago, Elys was the sole individual unable to finish the cycle.

Hugo was the first male in that line, ready to take his place as the host and director of the Exelis Lab's company. The case was that he and his mother were the only close relatives of the original host, Silvia Gold, who were of legal age. His nieces were too young, and the last living immediate adult female relative who still lived was his mother's older sister, Rebecca, but she did not have any descendants. Besides, she was too old to carry a symbiote since she was almost sixty-five and secluded in another country.

Estela, his mother, was also eligible to carry the symbiote. She was in the healthy age range but declined in her son's favor.

The Joining took place in one of the Exelis Labs' operating rooms, which was equipped with the latest technology. Leading the transfer was Doctor Theresa Graciano, the top surgeon at the Frontier Institute and a distant relative of Doctor Susan Graciano, the creator of the symbiotes. Rumors circulated that Doctor Theresa Graciano carried Susan's symbiote, the third host, on the line. However, the identity of those carrying symbiotes remained confidential, making it impossible to know for certain.

"Ready," said Dr. Graciano to the nurse, an old man with synthetic gray eyes, who nodded in response. She continued, "Mr. Sigman-Gold, you will feel sleepy. Count one to ten."

Hugo was numb before number six.

Dr. Graciano took the symbiote from the capsule. It could only survive for three months in it. The being was not captivating. Beauty was not as important as preserving consciousness in something close to immortality. The shape of the being was oval, around seven centimeters long, with a short appendage at one extreme, designed to be attached to the host's neural system. The skin was pale gray with reddish spots on its crest, the distinctive feature of these beings. Every symbiote had unique marks, like a fingerprint. These could be reddish, brown, yellow, gray, or black. Some had spotless skin. These were called albinos. All symbiotes relied on the host's blood flow for nourishment, as they had limited muscular activity.

The surgery lasted six hours, a process in which the neural system of the symbiote was attached to the base of his brain.

***

The following day, Hugo felt dizzy and could not sit on the bed. Doctor Graciano was at his side, checking the machines and controlling his progress.

"You're doing ok," she said. "It's normal if you feel some dizziness now. You'll regain much of your conscience and mobility in one hour."

"When will the Join be complete?" asked Hugo, anxious.

"Around a week," Dr. Graciano injected a stabilizer into the tube attached to Hugo's left arm. "Also, consider a rejection or a slower recovery. The joining is something we can't guarantee. We discussed that; do you remember?"

"I do."

The doctor stared at him with no emotion. "Sharing the genetic mark doesn't mean the symbiote will complete the Joining, especially in your case. You are the only male in a lineage of females.

"I must remind you that you didn't train." Her forehead showed disapproval. "It's not advisable to avoid it..."

"But during the consultation, the Counselors assured everything was going to be ok..."

"Yes, they did, Mr. Sigman-Gold," the doctor replied with a rebuff and followed, "If you ask me, I think nobody who is going to do a joining should dodge the training..."

"There was no time. After my sister..." Grasped Hugo, "Everything was so sudden..."

"I understand this symbiote is essential for your family's business. Lives and health matter too, Mr. Sigman-Gold. Elys was your twin. She gives you some advantage in this case."

"If not..." stammered Hugo.

"Considering that your family has no more healthy grown-up female relatives left," interrupted her, guessing Hugo's deduction. "Yes, we would lose the symbiote, and your nieces are not an option. They're too young. I hope this isn't the case, anyway. Your mother is still eligible, but she rejected the opportunity. Maybe that can change in the worst likely scenario."

Doctor Graciano left the room and Hugo's mother came after an hour. She looked delighted at the sight of his son awake. "She told me you're doing great."

"She mentioned a rejection..."

"Nonsense. Elys was your twin. You'll be fine. The company will be ok." Her mother touched his hand affectionately. "How are you feeling?"

"Fogged..."

"That's normal. For a few days, my sister Amelia felt like that, and the joining was successful. She ran the company for over thirty years with brilliant success. Now, it's your turn to follow the tradition."

"I always knew it was my destiny, Mother. However, Elys..." Hugo felt puzzled.

"Don't blame yourself. That nobody-George put those dumb social ideas in her mind, resulting in her suicide... What happened to Elys is entirely his fault. Changed the entire system...." buffed Estela while wiping away the tears with her fingers. "They should imprison him, although there's no proof of his guilt. The scrutiners found no abnormalities in the psychological screening during the investigation."

"We should put him under the behavior chip and seclude him in one of those Re-education centers," groaned Hugo, who was now more awake. "Turn George into a flesh android and pay for all he did to her... He deserves to work in the Telerium refinery until his last day."

"Relax, my son. You need to rest. He'll pay, don't worry." Estela smiled with wet eyes and a grin. "There are always other ways..."

"Symbiotes are the closest approach to immortality for humans. Science had limitations in preserving bodies beyond people's life expectancy, but it offered a means for our souls and minds to persist through time. Avoiding the reset that death brings us all."

Dr. Edith Perlman
Symbiotes and the Immortality of Consciousness
(2080)

FIVE

In under three weeks, two more than expected, Hugo made a full recovery. He returned to his new function as director on a Monday, ready to finish the unconcluded job Elys left while she held the same position.

He opened the door of Ely's office. The room appeared spacious with white walls and a tall ceiling adorned with oval lamps. A vast window faced the internal garden of the Exelis Lab Central, with a formidable tree in the middle adorned with flower buds. Silvia Gold, founder of Exelis Labs, planted a southern magnolia tree, now a huge specimen.

The glass of the window appeared new, with no stained pale curtains in sight. Everything seemed perfect in order except for a prominent vase showcasing withered jasmines on the desk, the dried petals adorning the glass surface. Nearby, a digital picture showed George smiling and holding his nieces.

"Nobody took proper care of this office?" groaned Hugo, putting his case on the desk with a loud bang. George's photo ruined his morning.

"I'm so sorry, Director, but Mrs. Estela Sigman-Gold didn't order the office to be cleaned," answered the room assistant.

"This mess is disgusting. Send a cleaner right away," Hugo said in a bitter tone.

"By all means, Director," said the voice.

After a few minutes, a synthetic janitor took away the vase containing the withered flowers and polished the desk's surface until it gleamed.

"Throw this into the garbage," ordered Hugo, handing the janitor the digital portrait. He then dismissed the cleaner with a brusque movement of his hand. The office improved without George's pictures or dead flowers. He also asked for a jar of mineral water placed over the desk. Everything was ready for Exelis Labs' new phase.

The new director relaxed in a chair; his mind fixated on the image he had created, a successful businessman bringing triumph to his family company.

He found himself on the verge of finalizing a deal with Ganimi Inc., the most prominent company from the outer settlements, and Exelis Labs would become the star company on Earth. Just like a pharmaceutical empire, they stood as the leading distributors of medications in most countries. A deal with Ganimi will equal Silvia Gold's achievements, the company's founder, which occurred over eighty years ago. She made Exelis Labs an essential part in medicine and the top brand worldwide. Since then, Exelis products have achieved renowned, and its technology served as a reference of quality for minor laboratories.

"I'm sorry to interrupt, director, but the executive of Gemini Inc. is here," said the assistant office. "Mrs. Elys scheduled this meeting a month ago."

"I know," said Hugo, impatient. "Let her in, please, and give her the usual welcome set... That stuff my sister used to do."

"By all means, director."

After a few minutes, a black woman arrived. Mrs. Kazya served as the Chief Technology Officer of Ganimi Inc., earning a reputation for her contracts with Earth companies and becoming famous for her sharp eye for good deals. Hugo felt nervous. He understood that this opportunity was extraordinary and could establish his name in the family if he succeeded.

Mrs. Kazya, in her prime, had long black locks tied in a

sophisticated hairstyle. Her designer clothes showcased simplicity and refinement, with a delicate hue of pale blue that stood out against her dark skin. She had on a fancy brooch with the logo of Ganimi Inc. on her chest, and in her left hand held her case and the bag with the welcome present in her left hand: some local sweets and fancy towels.

Mrs. Kazya displayed a haughty attitude. Her yellowish eyes sparkled when she fixed her gaze on him. He possessed a small stature, resembling the typical Earthling.

"Welcome, Mrs. Kazya," said Hugo with his best smile. He displayed charm whenever he desired.

"My pleasure, Mr. Sigman-Gold," she answered with a slight smile. "I hope you're ready to do business, because I have little time on the planet," she said.

"Certainly... Would you like something to drink or eat?"

"No, thank you. I already had my breakfast," Mrs. Kazya dismissed with a hand gesture. She sat down, opened the case, and took out a screen. "By the way, I'm sorry for your recent loss... My condolences."

"Thanks... Anyway, umm..." Hugo rubbed his forehead. A sudden anguish filled him, and a flash of broken glasses and flowers came to his mind. The red color clouded his sight. He shook her head, confused. In an instant, everything became white and polished once more.

"Are you ok?" asked her, curious.

Hugo put on his best smile. "I'm thirsty…" He filled a glass with mineral water, and he felt better. "You may continue, please."

"Well, according to your sister's reports," said Mrs. Kazya while reading on her screen, "Exelis Labs is developing this suppressor capable of reducing the stress and control loss for hours, and gives the potential consumer instant calm, and mental clarity… What's its name?"

"Anuxin, Mrs. Kazya. Exelis Labs is proud of this. My sister played a role in the team that developed the drug. She came up with the idea."

"Yes, I'm well informed about her profile… A talented pharmaceutical engineer with a Ph.D. in psychology and medicine and the former director of Exelis. Outstanding."

"She left quite an impression on people, yes…"

"However, I read her last report from a month ago. She had concerns regarding the side effects of Anuxin. Mrs. Sigman-Gold's reported that individuals have the potential to develop early dementia, tremors, cerebral cancer, violent behavior, loss of social empathy, hallucinations, and a high level of addiction after long-term drug intake."

"Yes, but only in rare cases," argued Hugo. "2% had those effects. 98% reacted with no problems in long-term trials. This potential can transform psycho-empathic therapies, and the possibility of profit has the potential to be beyond imagination."

"Yes, this could change many things," she agreed, leaving the screen on the desk, lacing her fingers. She paused for a long time, then continued, "I'm going to be blunt. This drug has huge potential. We're interested," she said with a grin.

Hugo had a good feeling but remained stolid. Mrs. Kazya went on, "Unlike your sister's approach with the product, Ganimi is not into therapies. Our company is considering this pill for laborers. Anuxin might boost productivity in our many Tellurium refineries on the planet. This is our perspective. What do you think?"

Hugo drew numbers in his mind. The profit would be huge, a complete success for Exelis Labs. The drug passed all trial stages and awaited final approval.

"Never thought about that possibility, but I think it's realistic," he beamed. "However, you understand we have a policy not to outsource. Exelis Labs should control the complete production."

"Those conditions are acceptable," she nodded. "However, we need more information concerning the side effects detailed in the reports. We look for a percentage between 0,5% to 1%. That 2% is below our standards. Solve that, and you'll have the contract."

"How much time does Ganimi require?"

"A month, Mr. Sigman-Gold. There are other labs, like HB Pharma, who are offering a similar product," She smiled, "However, Exelis Labs has a high reputation in the market, and is also the leading company. I hope you honor that prestige."

"We will," Hugo smiled and saw his golden future close at hand.

"Are symbiotes something near immortality? I call them a humankind abomination."

Perfect Patrick Becket
The Only Church of Jesus

(2100)

SIX

George and his daughters had a few weeks of relative peace. A calm that caused a slight uneasiness within him. The revelation of Ely's will fueled his anger, leaving him unable to fulfill her last wishes. They won, and the symbiote was still active, with part of her conscience in Hugo's mind. However, the girls' company made his day brighter. Their innocent laugh and holding them in his arms brought some happiness in those dark days.

He played with Rita and Ellen in the living room. It was a Saturday afternoon. They were on the rug, piling the plastic blocks, playing to make a tall tower, "which will reach the sky," according to Ellen's plan. George marveled his girls would not resign after the blocks fell. The twins would always rebuild, trying new ways, laughing, and clapping.

He experienced a sense of hopelessness. His daughters did not abandon the project despite the continual failure, like he did with Elys's last will. His eyes clouded with tears, and he hid his head between the knees.

He remembered the last memory of Elys. She had breakfast with him and the girls. She went to the Exelis Labs' office with the home android for maintenance, which seemed an obvious excuse. Elys shot herself in the head, fell through the wide window, and landed on the garden grass. She wanted to destroy the symbiote. Her failure was unknown to her and will remain so.

The image of Ely's body on the grass, surrounded by the flowers, would never leave George's memory. The grass fragrance could make him cry.

"Don't worry, Papa..." said Ellen, while piling up a new tower, looking at him with an intelligent gaze, followed with a bright smile. "Mamita is in heaven, Dad, she's taking care of us... She loves us."

Rita stopped piling blocks and put her tiny arms around her father's head. "We love you, Papa..."

The tears flooded his eyes, and he wished to cry forever and never stop.

"Master, Mr. Sigman-Gold is here," announced the droid, breaking the scene.

George refused to listen and was incapable of lifting his head. His gaze burned, and his throat was stiff as a stone.

He entered the room with his typical pride, fancy clothes, and head up. "We need to talk..." said Hugo in a bitter tone.

George dried his tears and stood up, leaving Rita close to her sister. "What is it?"

"Where are my sister's files?"

"I don't know what you are talking about, Hugo," George was having a rough day and was not in the mood for a fight with his brother-in-law.

"First, you wanted to destroy our family symbiote. It's not strange that you also wish to burn our business down to ashes ... Where are the files?"

After a few seconds, George smiled. "Are you referring to Ely's research? The Anuxin stuff?"

Hugo clenched his teeth. "Yes, the Anuxin project. Give me the files."

"They're gone forever. Elys knew you'd twist her research into some economic gain. She wanted Anuxin to help people, to improve their lives, not to make them mere machines to die for productivity quotas," George paused, "Elys destroyed everything..."

"I'll take them into my custody if you don't give me the

files."

George stared at him and looked at his daughters. He called the android. "Please, take the girls to their bedroom. Get them ready for bed. I'll go later for their bedtime story."

The robot followed instructions and departed alongside the girls. Only Hugo and George occupied the room.

"Don't you dare to take them away from me... I have custody, and I love them!" George gasped for breath. "Your only priority is money and success. You want to take them only to harm me? You don't give a damn about their happiness!"

"The files."

"I told you; Elys destroyed them... How many times do I have to repeat it?"

Hugo fixed his eyes on George's and recognized the wrinkle in the corner of his mouth almost curved into a hidden smile. George's green eyes sparkled like a child disguising a precious toy, as he used to do when he sensed remorse. Hugo kept looking at his face. He wished never to stop, not for disdain, but for delight. George's presence turned into something different, a familiar thrill. Euphoria overwhelmed Hugo, and a sense of bewilderment intensified in his chest. He took his eyes off and stared at the floor, embarrassed.

"You're not telling the truth," Hugo whispered, feeling ashamed, trying to feel the same level of hatred towards George as he did in the past.

Hugo was a man full of pride. He never whispered or showed embarrassment. But then, the always-confident Hugo Sigman-Gold vanished into the room.

"I've got to go..." said Hugo, leaving the house.

"Following the Joining, we recommend psycho-empathic therapy for hosts. The weight of previous consciousness can lead to psychological instability in the new host."

Dr. Alfred E. Giménez
Psychological Worldwide Association
(December 2102)

SEVEN

In the usual place, the luxurious Hotel Athenas, Hugo awaited his arrival. He lay on the bed, enveloped in a blue silk robe, gazing at the ceiling, anticipating a peaceful night. Solange emerged as the selected individual. She had the power to make him forget about his problems. But that night, he craved Jem. He needed him, especially that night. George's subtle smile made him nervous that afternoon. Since his sister introduced him years ago, he has despised him with all his heart. That emotion would persist. It appeared almost second nature to him to loathe George, as though it were a daily game. Those feelings seemed unclear now, evolving into something else.

Jem appeared, dressed in a fancy yellow suit with a smile, as the door creaked open. He served as a pleasure android, the best means to avoid diseases or unwanted pregnancies. Hugo never publicly ventured into relationships with men, mainly because of his family's religious beliefs rather than social judgment. Many decades ago, people didn't concern themselves with what others did in their bedrooms or with whom they married. However, Hugo's family, belonging to the minority, still held steadfast to their religious conviction - the creed of The Only Church of Jesus.

Hugo made a firm decision to never repeat his sister's mistake of marrying a stranger, which resulted in a tragic end for her. He had the responsibility to select a woman of his status to enhance the bloodline, then conceive children and transfer the symbiote to them.

Jem approached with his usual smile and lay down at his side, holding his head with his arm.

"How was your day, my love?" asked Jem, touching Hugo's cheek affectionately. The contact made Hugo feel aroused, but he waited.

"I'm stressed, Jem. A bad day," said George, looking at him. His black skin held a captivating beauty. His dark eyes glowed, and his body displayed a sculpted form, reminiscent of an obsidian statue.

"I'm going to fix that, darling... I know, and I always do."

Jem did it to Hugo, and then Hugo did it to Jem. When the dance began, the merging of the white and black skins created a striking contrast. The twilight cast peculiar shadows on the white walls. Over the black, the ginger hair glistened. Hands bonded, legs weaved, and breaths tied in one synchronized song. At the peak of ecstasy, Hugo screamed over Jem, moving his head vigorously back. When he fell on Jem, his face met George's breathless. George's mouth was open in deep pleasure, like he used to do every time they made it. Hugo's trembling hand touched George's lips, and he kissed his fingers, as usual.

"Are you ok, darling?" asked George, his light brown hair shining in the dim light. He stretched his arms, doing an arc with his slender back. His green eyes sank into Hugo's eyes.

Hugo blinked and scrubbed his eyes. His brother-in-law vanished, and Jem's sensual face appeared, looking at him worriedly. "Are you ok, sweetheart?" repeated in a seductive tone.

"Please, go... We're done for tonight," Hugo declared, purposefully avoiding Jem's gaze. He felt an intense sense of terror, preventing him from looking again and seeing George. Wishing for his presence made him mad. Jem disappeared from the room, and Hugo stayed there till dawn.

"Cellular memory held the key to creating symbiotes. It's hard to believe, but even a tiny drop of blood contains a piece of our consciousness. Our cells don't just preserve energy, they also carry the essence of our existence."

Dr. Susan Graciano
The Survival of Human Conscience
(2047)

EIGHT

"I don't understand why you have so many doubts, dear... You used to be more determined," said Estela. "It's quite simple that you have to do, and you know that."

Hugo stared at his mother. She visited his office, as she did with Elys when she was director, ensuring all was well in the company.

Hugo looked at his desk and realized something was missing on the surface.

"There used to be a portrait here..." he whispered to himself, then he drummed his fingers on the surface of the desk.

"You're not saying anything…" she complained, raising her voice. Then she sipped her coffee and bit into a biscuit. Hugo returned from his thoughts and noticed her presence.

"Sorry, mother. What were you saying?"

"You're distracted, my dear," Estela smiled at her son, "Your major goal was to bring success to Exelis. You've always been jealous of Elys… And I remember you talking so much about how you'd be better than her for the company's future. It's time to prove yourself right."

"I can't feel jealous of Elys. She let herself to be defeated by stupid ideas," he replied and regretted his words. He scrubbed his forehead and tried to breathe. Lately, he has been experiencing a disconnection in all his thoughts. He even had dreams of the initial host, Silvia Gold, speaking to him about the company deals. Sometimes, the Filippa host, his grandmother, demonstrated to Hugo her own memories of the childbirth process of Estela, his own mother, with all the physical pain and experience of euphoria at once.

"You must present the new results to Ganimi in two weeks…" she insisted.

"Mother, please, shut the fuck up…" mumbled him.

Estela showed no signs of surprise and continued to enjoy her coffee. "Now, you're talking like your sister with those rude words. I know you don't mean it. She learned those questionable manners from him... Before George, she was a lady," she took another bite of the biscuit, "You shouldn't let your sister's lousy behavior control you. Remember to take only the best of her, like her negotiation abilities and her charm."

"It's easy to say that... You don't have a symbiote inside you. Maybe I need psycho-empathic therapy, after all."

"Quit all that gibberish... That's for weak people," said Estela with contempt. "It seems you just need to take the girls away from him. He'll be desperate and give you the files. I know he has them. After all, he wants to destroy the company. Do you want to leave a positive footprint in Exelis or not?"

"I want to, I do..." sighed Hugo. Briefly, he had a feeling of being present. He regained his true self in the room, free from any intruding memories. He visualized himself as a successful director again. His parents were proud of him and everything he had achieved, patting his shoulder.

Hugo laced his fingers and saw his mother. He felt guilty. She was always there for him, and he failed her. She was the one who supported him when he received the symbiote before the Institute of Symbiosis, and it was she who used her influence to bypass all the mandatory training for the Joining.

"I should have trained, mother..." Hugo said, and his forehead frowned. "Elys did it, and she was ok. I never saw her struggling with all these... conflicts. She bonded easily with the symbiote..."

"Nonsense! You're a tough person, my son," said she with a charming smile, "And I know you'll overcome all this."

"I hope so..."

"My dear, George hates us. Don't let Ely's feelings for him confuse you. She loved him, you don't," she reminded him with a sharp gaze. "He'll do anything for those girls. I'm sure you know that. You have the resources in front of you. Can't you see them?"

Hugo stared at her, feeling a fleeting whisper in his mind, chilling like a breeze. He could feel Elys' hatred towards their mother—the frustration that derived from her mother's rejection towards George, feeling loneliness, all the complaints, never feeling that she was enough. His goals were so close to materializing with only determination.

"I can see them, mother..."

***

George was making a pair of boots for a customer. Despite having sufficient funds for life, the business thrived. However, George enjoyed making shoes. It was a way to be busy and remember Elys and how they met, keeping a part of his identity present daily.

The girls were in daycare at midday. The modest place

was called "Kids & Fun." He wanted his daughters to interact with regular people. It was Ely's wish also, since she always felt weird outside her social class. He abandoned the incomplete boots and headed to the kitchen. He was in the mood to make carrot muffins for the girls. They loved those with tea and some lemon.

He could cook fancy recipes, like croissants and a good roasted chicken, but the girls loved the simple carrot muffins with a sugar glaze on the top.

While George finished the glaze, the doorbell rang many times. He waited for the droid to open. The sound persisted, and then he recalled the robot's order to collect the girls.

George opened the door, and Hugo was there, dressed in fancy clothes.

"Hi, Hugo..." said George, surprised. "I told you to give me notice if..."

"I'm not here to see my nieces, George," Hugo's tone was icy.

"What do you need?"

"May I enter?"

George let him enter and went to the kitchen.

"Would you like a cup of tea?"

"No, thanks, my visit will be short." He was too stiff, his eyes too rigid, in total control—the old Hugo.

George brewed tea and sat at the table. He stared at him with a mug between his hands. It was freezing outside. "What is it?"

"I'm here to take the girls into custody," said Hugo without spinning.

George left the mug on the table; his fingers trembling.

"What did you say?" muttered George, livid, his wide green eyes open.

"I have a legal order to take my nieces. You're no longer suitable to take care of them."

"I have their custody!" George shouted. His green eyes blurred with tears. "Why are you doing this? I left your family alone, just as you all wanted..."

"I want the files," said Hugo. "I know you have them."

George dried the tears with a paper towel and tried to recover. He observed Hugo. He was too silent. Something was wrong with him. During the last visit, George's intense gaze reminded him of how Elys used to look at him. Now, he was like a hollow shell with no emotions, stiff like a statue.

"You had Anuxin..."

"That's none of your business, George."

"The drug is not ready, and it's meant for people with mental issues..."

"If you don't hand me the files, George, I'll take my nieces today."

"Elys told me that Anuxin was not ready yet... It was her own project to help people. We used to talk for hours about this," sobbed George when recalling the memory of her. "Anuxin was important to her. You're using it wrong!"

The main door opened, and the girls ran to the kitchen, excited about the muffin scent perfuming the house. With backpacks on its back, the droid appeared afterwards. George pretended he was cleaning the mug, trying to relax and not to scare his daughter, especially Rita, sensitive to his father's mood.

"The little ladies did excellent in the class, master," informed the droid.

George remained on his back, "It's ok, we'll talk about the girls later. You can finish your duties," ordered George, trying to remain calm. He turned, smiled, and turned his attention to his daughters. "I did this for you, my damitas," he gave a carrot muffin to each of them. They giggled, excited.

"Are we having tea with Uncle Hugo?" asked Rita, who was looking at them with a curious gaze.

"No, my darling, he's not staying..." answered George. Words almost got stuck in his throat. "He needs to attend to some business. He's a busy man."

Ellen took a muffin and approached her uncle. She gave him a bright smile.

"This is for you..." she laughed and ran into his father's arms, who hugged her, kissing her forehead.

Hugo held the muffin, confused for an instant. Then, he stared at George, "You have until midnight."

"The training for the joining, also known as preparation, makes the process endurable by providing the new host with the skills and tools necessary to overcome all the challenges of merging with the previous consciousness."

Institute of Symbiosis
Training Manual & General Recommendations
(2070)

NINE

Anuxin had an extraordinary effect. Hugo had no sensation when he confronted George. He was the old Hugo Sigman-Gold; cold, determined, and relentless. During the drug reaction, which lasted hours, all the other voices fell silent. He thought he had perceived a subtle whisper for a moment. However, he could crush it.

He was now in his luxurious penthouse, drinking red wine, a new craving, waiting for George to surrender. He sensed he was close to the ultimate victory.

The screen displayed the legal order. Hugo's mother used some of her influences, which were easy to get with the correct amount of credit.

His mother entered the penthouse; his father accompanied her. Both wore fancy clothes.

"Is everything ready, my son?" asked Estela.

"Yes, mother. Tonight, all will be done. We'll have everything set up for the deal with Ganimi by next week."

His father smiled, then frowned. "However, taking the girls from him... isn't it too harsh? I feel bad for them." He shook his head, worried.

"Raul, you're just like Elys... Too sentimental," she scolded, with disdain. "We're only defending what is ours... Nothing more."

"I know this deal is important, but... The girls, they may suffer," Raul argued with a sense of guilt.

"My dear husband, that is nonsense. He'll give us the files for the girls," said Estela, confident. "He likes to play rebellious, but he's just a coffee shop revolutionary. Nothing else..."

"Yes, but..." started Raul again.

"He's a nobody, my dear. We must ensure everything is under our power. Never undervalue the weak..."

"Where are you going?" asked Hugo, tired of his parents' argument.

"We're going to this charity event for orphans. They're

from this south country, The Federation. You can join us later. Since you are the new director, it's a good idea to attend," suggested Estela.

"Mother..."

"Don't push the boy, Estela." groaned his father, "There will be many events to attend in the future. Now, he must focus on 'solving' this problem."

"You're right, my dear. We should go."

Hugo checked his watch. It was almost time. He took his jacket, and before leaving, he grabbed the muffin. He was hungry. The treat looked lovely, and something familiar made him smile. He gave it a bite. The mixture of orange zest, carrots, and brown sugar made him smile. Flavors he loved from the first time George made the muffins for her. While taking another bite, he heard laughter coming from his kitchen. Although he frowned, he was not concerned. He ate the muffin completely in seconds. Hugo observed the large living room window. Elys' reflection appeared on the glass, with her long ginger hair and mischievous smile. She looked at her own hands. They were delicate, with long beautiful fingers. A simple silver circle on her ring finger, a gift from George in the second year of their relationship.

She went to the kitchen and blinked before the bright morning light. Elys was in the forest house, and George was making carrot muffins. Something moved inside her, making her hands touch her belly. She was pregnant; the twins were almost due, and she was craving those muffins.

George was there, decorating the muffins with sugar glaze, biting his lower lip, and concentrating on the task, making perfect spirals. George smiled at her when he noticed her presence, and she perceived the connection through his green eyes. Love, peace, friendship, and tenderness emanated from him. They became one when they looked at each other.

Hugo woke up on the floor, shuddering, with a trail of carrot muffin crumbles on his chest. Abruptly, he woke up and brushed off the crumbs. Fear overwhelmed him. He touched his stomach, feeling a mixture of disappointment and relief. It was his body again.

"I've got to finish this, once and for," he thought, leaving the penthouse.

"Symbiotes created from males are better for male hosts. Female-made ones are preferable for female hosts. The preference is not arbitrary, but based on hormonal balance, socialization, and the stability of the joining. Is it possible to transfer male Symbiotes to a female host and vice versa? The answer is yes, but adaptation's success rate is low."

Arinna Smithson, Ph.D.
Symbiotes Joining Issues Research
(September 2099)

TEN

George leaped from his chair upon hearing a loud bang at midnight. He was asleep, and a mug of lukewarm tea spilled on the table when he moved his arm.

Hours felt endless agony for him. He wished he didn't have to decide between keeping Ely's promise to destroy the symbiote or keeping his daughters sleeping after he read them their favorite story, "The Golden Bird."

The droid opened the door, and Hugo burst into the kitchen like a storm.

"Well, did you decide?" he shouted, banging his hands over the table. His face was as red as his hair, now all messy.

George opened his mouth in disbelief. In all the eight years he had known him, he had never seen him like that. Hugo had an insane gaze, his lips trembling and the color of the cheeks too pale. The Anuxin's effect was gone.

"Yes, I did…" George said, "However, I want to ask you something… Why are you so obsessed with Ely's project?"

"Shut up! Give me the files!" yelled Hugo, his forehead covered in sweat. Hugo's face grew paler, and as a result, his eyes became bloodshot.

"No," George was adamant, his soothing voice contrasting Hugo's. "Answer me… At least you owe me that. You may have all your family power, but this is my house. You'll have to respect that. There are still laws that would call this situation a property assault."

"My sister was a coward! She was against us; she tried to kill our symbiote and destroy the family business."

"Take that back…" said George in a low voice containing rage.

"What are you going to do? Call the police?" Hugo's laugh continued for long seconds.

George sighed and looked at him. He lacked the energy to continue arguing.

"Don't speak ill of Elys. She didn't kill herself because she was a coward... You would know if you had done the training," explained George. He was holding back the tears, trying to keep himself together. "She knew pursuing a claim to end the symbiote was useless, so she did that. Your mother would put a lot of money into taking her petition down... So, she took that path. She felt pushed by her own family..."

"No, she chose that path because you made her hate our family... Those communitarian ideas..."

"Did she? Perhaps you should navigate in her conscience," George inspected Hugo's face, "From your expression, I can tell you don't believe a word you just said..."

Hugo clenched his teeth and pushed the table some centimeters away from him. "I can denounce you for stealing company information, George..." threatened Hugo with a crazy smile, avoiding George's logic. His brown eyes were wide open.

"Yes, I thought you'd say that. You're just like your parents. You threaten people if they don't fulfill your petition on a whim."

"The files!" shouted Hugo. George crossed his arms and fixed his green eyes on him. A stare that made Hugo's knees shake. He hated him, and he adored his lovely face with that curly hair and sensual lips. Hugo covered his face with his hands. He felt lost.

"You should have never carried that symbiote, Hugo... You didn't train, and it was your mother who paid for this suffering. And it was a fortune for sure," George whispered, "Did you know she was the primary candidate to carry the symbiote before Elys?"

"Nonsense! She declined in my favor! You're a liar!" shouted him, with his face in his palms, now turning his back.

"Do you still believe all your mother's stories, Hugo?" George felt surprised. "She declined because she had a terrible relationship with her mother, the previous host to Elys, your grandmother, Filippa. She chose not to confront that situation. It was too painful for her. She could have done psycho-empathic therapy and heal the pain. However, she liked the easy way, and throw the 'thing' to your sister before you."

"Shut up!" cried Hugo with desperation.

The kitchen remained silent, and George only heard Hugo's speeding up breath.

George stood up, "Come with me..." ordered George.

"No!"

"I said come with me!" reiterated with a not so soothing tone, "I want to show you something."

Hugo was still silent. George approached him and took his sweaty hand with care, as at any moment his brother-in-law could break into pieces. Hugo resisted for some seconds. Then he let George guide him. The touch of George's hands made him remember the past times when Elys crossed fingers with him and made love, then kissed and laughed. Hugo whined like a wounded animal, holding tears; the pain inside him was unbearable, feeling broken and surrounded by voices flashing in his head.

They moved upstairs and crossed a lengthy hallway. George stopped in front of a door and opened it. The half-light of the corridor showed Rita and Ellen sleeping in a room decorated with flowers on the walls.

"Do you see them?" asked George in a quiet voice, smiling at his sleeping daughters.

Hugo lifted his head. They looked very peaceful. Rita was hugging his elephant plushie, and Ellen was holding one of her dinosaur books. Both men approached the beds. The twin's ginger hair made Hugo touch George in a reflex.

"I would never exchange them for the files, Hugo," continued George, still looking at his girls. "You can have them and finish your deal. I don't care," he paused and lowered his head, "Today I realized I was fighting to fulfill Ely's last desire, which was to destroy the symbiote and your vile family. Then, I realized it's not my fight anymore. Sometimes, other people's fights are not ours. I thought about that for the past hours, during the afternoon..."

George took a small, rounded device out of his pocket. He gave it to Hugo. "Here are Ely's files, Hugo. Do what you must. Now you're free to become a successful businessman, just like you have always wanted. Now you can sell Anuxin to some ruthless company. I prefer that before risking my daughters. That'd be a pain they will never forget. I can't change the world."

Hugo's hand quivered. He saw the device in his hand. His mouth had a bitter taste, and the smile turned into a straight line drawn by stiff lips. That moment became an eternity of torment for him.

"When I look at them, I only know they are my entire world. Giving up my girls for the sake of a company's profits is simply not worthwhile. Even if profits bring more misery to the world. Some fights have limits..."

The quietness grew as a high wall between them.

"Can I say goodbye to them?" Hugo asked in an outburst, his eyes shining like Elys.

"Just try not to wake them, ok? They have school tomorrow," said George.

Familiarity with the minor details of the cozy and simple room grew on him. Among the family photos on the screens, there were also the toys George made for them, including the wooden pony that Ellen used to ride. A mixture of lavender and plain soap filled the air in the place.

Hugo approached the beds in silence. He first kissed Rita on the forehead and touched her hand, trying not to break into pieces. Then he caressed Ellen's hair. It was silky and red. In that touch, he saw them through Ely's eyes. He experienced a deep bond with them. The sense of adoration, of them as if they were a part of her own flesh and blood, her intimate creation. Not being able to talk to her girls as their mother anymore created a feeling of emptiness inside him. All echoes of another life lived resonating in his body as a terrible song.

Hugo fled from the room and went downstairs, scared and agitated. When he was in the middle of the stairs, George called him. He paused, glancing at George with confusion, as if the voices in his head had returned.

"Promise me something…"

Hugo opened his mouth to say something, but he went silent.

"Never again threaten my daughters… is that clear?"

Hugo nodded and disappeared.

"In the past, one out of four hosts committed suicide. Nowadays, this rate stands at one in ten, showing a significant improvement. The key to achieving a successful bond between the host and the symbiote lies in thorough training, the preparation."

Dr. Theresa Graciano
Frontier Institute
(2120)

ELEVEN

The office door opened. A woman's face appeared before the big panel. "Director Sigman-Gold?"

Hugo held a glass of wine, gazing into emptiness. The room was dark, but a beam of daylight shone over him. The director was stiff as a statue. His face was thinner and pale, with dark circles under his eyes.

"Director Sigman-Gold?" asked the woman again. She was wearing white overalls.

"What is it?" he asked, fixing his eyes on her in a reflex that she jumped.

"I'm here to communicate that Anuxin is ready for the final stage. We lowered the secondary effects to 0,6%," she announced, concerned and scared about his aspect.

Hugo took a sip from his glass of wine and smiled without joy. "That's excellent news, isn't it?"

"Do you want to check everything in the lab?" she asked.

"That won't be necessary... Just send me the final report through my office assistant. Now."

The woman left. Hugo looked at the magnolia tree through the wide glass. It was in full bloom, with all the white flowers open, yet its view made him sad and depressed.

He felt empty after leaving George's house, as if he was losing something dear again. Since then, he used Anuxin daily, which helped him silence the whispers in his head. But it was only a palliative. As the effect faded, the madness grew stronger, like a relentless weed. He could not sleep, and sometimes he thought other people with blurry faces were surrounding him. He considered psycho-empathic therapy as a solution. However, that idea died before he could take any action.

That morning, he had an Anuxin dose. It was the old version, a previous formula. The effect vanished at midday, and his mind filled with the former host's past lives. Tired of fighting against his own mind and others', Hugo longed for peace. He was thinner, with no strength in his body.

Hugo even secluded some days in Ely's old house in the forest after his mother pushed him about the Anuxin situation. She was pleased when he knew about the file retrieval, and she became obsessed with the Ganimi deal.

Hugo opened the drawer of his desk and saw the neuro stick. He had always had it since he was a teenager. He used it for self-defense when he went to the Athenas hotel for his encounters with Jem and Solange. That place was fancy but also full of mafia gangs. He used the neuro stick only once, when he needed to paralyze a big guy who wanted to start a fight. The device had a cylinder shape, with a rounded end and intensity controls at the bottom.

Hugo put the weapon on the desk and opened the wide glass through his implant. A strong magnolia scent permeated the office. The neuro-stick power setting was at its maximum level. A silent atmosphere enveloped the office, accompanied by a sense of emptiness. Only the sound of the wind going through the window broke the vacuum.

The screen on the desk displayed the Anuxin report. Hugo skimmed it and smiled. After all, he achieved something. He would leave his footprint at Exelis Labs. Profits will soar with the Ganimi deal, thanks to Anuxin.

Hugo thought about the emptiness haunted him after he left George's house, as if he was once again parting with something cherished.

His eyes blurred with tears as he started laughing. The voices were screaming in his mind. They were all saying different things, like an out-of-tune choir. Some of them referred to business, the company, others referred to family conflicts and body pains and pleasure.

He pulled out the last Anuxin pill from his pockets. It was orange, wrapped in blue and transparent plastic. His hand trembled, and in a moment of clarity, he knew it was too late and he tossed the pill out the window, filled with rage. The drug will ease the agony for some hours, then the voices will surround him, lurking at him. The riot in his mind will stay for hours, preventing him from eating, sleeping, or engaging in a normal conversation.

He breathed, closed his eyes, and placed the neuro stick on his right temple. He pushed the button, and the dark embraced him.

"What's the sense of symbiotes? Merely a way to hold on to the past. This only brings misery to the hosts, since it means that each new one carries a bigger box filled with old memories, fights, and pain. Eternity does not suit humans."

Roland Edward Shuls
UIJ Philosophy chair
(2112)

TWELVE

Estela Sigman-Gold shook the hand of Mrs. Kazya, the CEO of Ganimi Inc. The new Exelis Director wore a lavish suit with a pearl necklace, her hair combed in a neat bun. A vase held fresh magnolias on the desk. Next to it, there is a screen with a photo of her with Elys, Hugo and her husband, Raul.

"It is a pleasure, Mrs. Sigman-Gold," greeted Mrs. Kazya, releasing Estela's hand and sitting on the chair. "We'll make the deal right away. However, before we start, may I ask something?"

"By all means, Mrs. Kazya," said Estela, while sipping coffee.

"What happened to your son? I was expecting him today. The last time we spoke, he was eager to close this deal with Ganimi."

"He had some health issues, and now I'm taking his position," Estela smiled.

"I understand." Mrs. Kazya took her screen out of the case that was lying on the desk. "We received the last report from your son two days ago. Ganimi is excited about the previous results and ready to close the deal."

"That's wonderful," Estela said with crossed fingers. "I already read the terms, and so did our legal department. They gave us the green light." She smiled at Mrs. Kazya and her eyes sparkled, full of ambition. "This is not official yet. But I'm thrilled to inform you that Anuxin will be ready for release in roughly one month."

"That's two months earlier than expected. I see that your company's excellent reputation is very well-based, Mrs. Sigman-Gold."

Estela smiled and touched her pearl necklace while rocking in the chair. "Indeed, we're the best."

That afternoon, they sealed the deal in which Exelis Lab would provide Anuxin for the Telerium refineries on Earth for ten years, with the possibility of renovating the contract after its expiration. Exelis Labs was now the leading company on Earth and the outer settlements.

***

Estela made her way to the Re-education Center that night before the celebration in the company — it was a tall square building with white walls and rounded windows.

One supervisor, a droid from the International Robotic Industry, the IRI, guided her. "Mrs. Sigman-Gold, you may enter," said the android and opened a door. Entering, she saw her son lying on a table in the room. She was wearing a white gown. Then she noticed that a doctor was leaning over him.

"How is he?" asked Estela.

The woman took some seconds to answer. She completed stitching Hugo's left side, then gazed at Estela with her artificial gray eyes. "He's stable, and the symbiote is out of danger. The psycho-suppressor is working, so the symbiote is asleep now."

"Perfect. May I have some words with him before the activation?" asked Estela.

The doctor nodded and left. Estela approached and saw his son, her own blood. Hugo had the same ginger hair as Ely's, and they both inherited it from her. Unfortunately, neither of them coped with the responsibility. She frowned, feeling disappointed.

Hugo opened his eyes and saw his mother looking at

him. The light hurt his eyes, and he blinked and creased his eyelids in pain.

"Mother, where am I?" asked him, confused. No voices echoed in his head anymore. After so many weeks of whispers and ghosts, he was himself again.

"You are in the Re-education Center, my dear," she answered. "My boy, I knew you will try to hurt yourself, and it's time for you to heal... After all, you carry important company property."

"You replaced my neuro-stick?" Hugo tried to get up, and a pair of plastic belts kept him down. "What does this mean? Mother?" He shook his arms with no energy.

"You and your sister may be my children, but neither of you is cold-blooded enough to run our business," she tried to hold back the tears. "This breaks my heart... But you left me no choice, darling. I couldn't let this happen again. I tried to advise you."

Hugo got silent. His eyes were wide open, and they were staring at his mother. "Will you do this to me? A prison for life like a damned flesh android? Carry the symbiote for me, please..." He begged.

She set eyes on his only living son and shook her head. "No, I can't. I'm too old."

"That's not true. You're fifty-one, you're still eligible..."

"I won't…"

"George was right then… You didn't want the symbiote because of your issues with your mother!" exclaimed Hugo in a rage.

"You don't know what you are talking about, Hugo," said Estela, with contained anger. She only used his name when disappointed. "You didn't know my… mother. My sister Amelia would always say the nicest things about her. After all, she was Filippa's favorite. However, I was the smartest of the three sisters. I was her last resort, always backing Amelia in the business. Do you think I wanted that?"

"You could train… There are options…" Hugo's eyes flooded with tears. The desperation ate him little by little, as he longed to escape the lives that had never belonged to him.

"The training?" she laughed, bitter. "It takes almost five years. I'll be too old by then. No, the company has decided, and I have here the legal instrument. You'll keep the symbiote alive until my granddaughters come of age, train, and carry the symbiote themselves. Meanwhile, I'll run the company."

"We could transfer the symbiote to another person… Please, mother…"

"And contaminate the symbiote with the wrong people?" she clicked her tongue. "Who? George?"

"He would never approve of the idea of joining any of the girls with the symbiote... He will fight to death for them," warned Hugo, furious.

"George is nobody. And don't worry. I'll take care of that matter, as I always do."

"You're not my mother... No mother does this to her children."

"I am your mother. And I'm doing this to protect you and our family. Sometimes, we must make sacrifices. I sacrificed and worked hard. Exelis is the greatest company on Earth. Your sister contributed. You did when you retrieved the files. I only ask a little more. You're young enough..."

"Don't do this to me... I beg you, do it for the love you have for me..." Hugo whispered.

"You don't have to worry, my dear. I promise the best for you, and you will regain freedom soon. Nothing that psyco-empathic therapy can't solve. I guarantee everything will be comfortable." She smiled and caressed his cheek. "We won't forget your sacrifice."

Estela kissed Hugo's forehead and left. When she was close to the hall, she heard him screaming and screaming again. They connected Hugo's re-education chip to her implant a few minutes later. This would allow her to watch him and take proper care of him. She could also command him to have an orderly life, make him eat nutritious food, shower, and attend events. Passing through the door, she smiled at the sight of the tall building. The company and her family were out of danger.

By the end of the year, Anuxin's profit would have risen to millions.

THE AUTHOR

Edle Julve was born in the small province of Tucuman, Argentina in 1985. She embarked on her literary journey at 12, guided by her dedicated high school teacher, José María Vera. Nurtured by her parents' love for reading and writing, she found solace and inspiration in the captivating worlds of science fiction and fantasy. After years of dedicated effort, Edle Julve published some works, including a tale in the sci-fi anthology, "Coplas Intergalácticas & Otros Yuyos" (Kala Publishing, 2020), "El Efecto Pigmalión" (Amazon, 2021), "The Harvest" (Amazon, 2023") and "La Ascensión" (Amazon, 2023). With an adventurous spirit, she continues to explore the realms of storytelling, sharing her passion with readers.

www.ingramcontent.com/pod-product-compliance
Lightning Source LLC
LaVergne TN
LVHW041749190726

843493LV00008B/2522